ALEUTIAN SPARROW

ALSO BY KAREN HESSE

Stowaway

Witness

A Light in the Storm

Just Juice

Out of the Dust

The Music of Dolphins

A Time of Angels

Phoenix Rising

Lavender

Sable

Letters from Rifka

Wish on a Unicorn

FOR YOUNGER READERS

The Stone Lamp

Poppy's Chair

Lester's Dog

ALEUTIAN SPARROW

KAREN HESSE

MARGARET K. MCELDERRY BOOKS
New York London Toronto Sydney

Margaret K. McElderry Books
An imprint of Simon & Schuster Children's
Publishing Division
1230 Avenue of the Americas
New York, New York 10020
Book design by Lee Wade
The text for this book is set
in Golden Cockerel.
The illustrations for this book are linocuts.

Manufactured in the
United States of America
10 9 8 7 6 5 4 3 2
Library of Congress
Cataloging-in-Publication Data
Hesse, Karen.
Aleutian sparrow / Karen Hesse.— 1st ed.
p. cm.
Summary: An Aleutian Islander
recounts her suffering during
World War II in American internment
camps designed to "protect"
the population from
the invading Japanese.
ISBN 0-689-86189-3
1. Aleuts—Juvenile fiction. [1. Aleuts—
Fiction. 2. Racially mixed people—Fiction.
3. World War, 1939–1945—Fiction.
4. Concentration camps—Fiction.] I. Title.
PZ7.H4364Al 2003
[Fic]—dc21   2003001338

ACKNOWLEDGMENTS

The following people contributed significantly to my understanding of this complex story: Charlotte Glover, Dave Kiffer, Clifford Homan, Gordon Zerbetz, Fay Schlais, Bob Newell, June Allen, Barbara Svarny-Carlson, and most especially Ray Hudson. Thank you.

In addition I thank Randy Hesse, Kate Hesse, Rachel Hesse, Liza Ketchum, Eileen Christelow, Bob MacLean, Tink MacLean, Wendy Watson, Hilary Goodman, Sharon Creech, and Brenda Bowen for their patient and wise counsel.

Finally I would like to thank the booksellers at Parnassus Books and the enthusiastic students, librarians, and educators I met while visiting Southeast Alaska.

FOR THE UNANGAX̂,

THE PEOPLE OF THE

ALEUTIAN AND

PRIBILOF ISLANDS

ALEUTIAN ISLANDS

Attu Island

Kiska Island

Atka Island

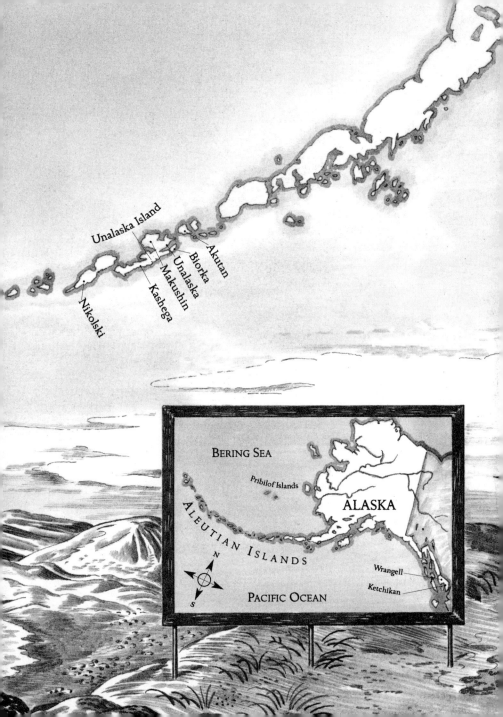

Unalaska Island

Biorka

Akutan

Unalaska

Makushin

Kashega

Nikolski

BERING SEA

Pribilof Islands

ALASKA

ALEUTIAN ISLANDS

N

S

PACIFIC OCEAN

Wrangell

Ketchikan

ALEUTIAN SPARROW

I noticed a string of strange, bare mountains rising out of the sea along the northern horizon. They resembled heaps of smoking slag; the sun, striking their sides, gave them a greenish cast like verdigris on copper. I asked a fellow passenger what they were. "Illusions," I thought he said, but now I realize he said they were Aleutians.

—Corey Ford, *Where the Sea Breaks Its Back*

Kashega

May–June 1942

Summer in Kashega

The old ones, Alexie and Fekla, they say,
"Go, Vera. Go to Kashega. See your mother, your friends.
It is only for the summer," they say.
"Go. Nothing will happen to us."

So I go, eager to visit Kashega,
Riding the mail boat out of Unalaska Bay
        as Alexie and Fekla Golodoff,
        and our snug house in Unalaska village,
        and my photographs and books, my little skiff,
And my twelve handsome chickens,
All fade into the fog.

WHAT WAR?

I arrive in Kashega. My friends Pari and Alfred squabble over me
    like a pair of seagulls fighting for a crab claw.
    My mother greets me like a stranger, with an
    Americanchin hug, then touches my hair.
There is no sign of trouble here. We have crayon days,
    big and happy.
The windows sparkle at night.
I had forgotten how a lighted window shines
    without blackout paper.

THE JAPANESE

They weren't always our enemy. There was a time when the
      Japanese sailed in and their crews played baseball with
      our Aleut teams.
But we saw what they were up to. We warned our
      government about Japanese who charted our
      shorelines, who studied our harbors from their fishing
      boats.
Our Japanese visitors expected always
      an amiable Aleut welcome. But
      when the hand of friendship was withdrawn,
They took their measurements and made their calculations
      anyway.

Life in Kashega

In the beginning, when I first moved away to Unalaska village
　　　to live with Alexie and Fekla Golodoff, I longed for
　　　Kashega. Kashega winter, when the men trap the blue
　　　fox. Kashega summer, when they
　　　hire themselves out to take the fur seal off the
　　　Pribilofs. All the Kashega year, with
　　　the boats bringing home sweet duck and fat sea lion.
Kashega autumns splash with salmon swimming into traps to
　　　become a winter of dry fish.
Sometimes sheep to shear, sometimes driftwood on the
　　　beach, sometimes an odd job.
And always Solomon's little store, lit by kerosene, where the
　　　men drink salmonberry wine and solve the problems
　　　of our people.

SOLOMON'S STORE

Zachary Solomon ran the Kashega store for ten years maybe.
But when the Japanese attacked Pearl Harbor,
      Zachary Solomon went to war.
Always a white man has run the store.
But my mother took over when Zachary Solomon left.
      And she likes it.

Hot-Spring Memory

"Remember," I ask my mother, "how we visited Akutan
And walked the path up into the hills,
      passing the boiling springs, climbing higher, to where
      blossoms framed the steaming pools like
      masses of perfumed hair?
"Remember," I ask my mother, "how we waded in?
      Could we go again?"
"Maybe," she says, never looking up, lost
      in the pages of *Life*.

MY MOTHER

My mother never talks about when she was young and she
     did not listen to the old ways to keep a man safe.
     How she closed her ears to the Aleut tales.
She never talks about how she met and fell in love with and
     married a white man, how she sent him to sea without
     a seal-gut coat. She never talks about the storms
     driving in and piling up the waves. How time after
     time she watched from the headlands, fighting the
     winds, waiting for my father's boat to come in.
She never says how I waited beside her, my fist crushing the
     seam of her skirt.
And she never, never talks about the day my father did not
     come home.

Even the Storms

Pari and I sit in the new spring grass watching a storm
    approach from the distance. "Have
    you missed Kashega?" she asks.
I nod, remembering the welcoming kitchens, the Christmas
    star of wood and glass,
The way our laughter crackled on winter nights like sugar
    frosting, the smell of our skin after a day gathering
    wildflowers in the summer hills.
Pari pulls me up with both hands, and we race to her house
    down the mountain path, wind walls rising around us,
    rain filling the gray cheeks of the sky.

WHITE ORCHID

"Last summer," I remind Pari as we dry off in her kitchen.
    "Last summer you led the way, carrying the fish
    basket to the far side of the lake.
    And we gathered bulbs of white orchid."
Pari says, "And Alfred's mother boiled the bulbs for us,
    and we rolled them in pools of warm fat
    and ate them with our fingers."
We lick our lips, remembering, and Pari combs out her
    hair and mine, and we promise to dig orchids
    again this August
When I get back with Alfred's family from fish camp.

Pari

She is more like my mother than I will ever be.
She likes all things cheechako.
She is only part Aleut, as I am, her father, like mine,
    a white man.
But while I like to sit with Alfred's family
    listening to the old stories,
    Pari prefers the store and my mother
    and the pages of the Sears and Roebuck catalog.

My Work

I was six when I stood outside Alfred's grandfather's house,
  where the old ways steep like tea in a cup of hours.
  Alfred's mother opened the door and gazed down
  at my small fists hanging by my sides.
  She understood my wanting. She said
  I could live in her house sometimes if I needed.
Eva, her daughter, dressed and fed me. She carried me on her
  hip like a big doll. Alfred, her son, taught me to fish
  and to row a skiff. The family taught me their stories.
I grew up seeing my mother every day, but spending most
  of my time in Alfred's house.
"Your work, Vera," Alfred's grandfather told me
  before I moved to Unalaska village,
  "your work is to know the ways of our people."
  I am good at my work.

Why I Left Kashega in the First Place

Not enough children to keep the school open.
And after my father died, I never listened to my mother.
Alexie and Fekla Golodoff, the old man and woman from
      Unalaska village,
They lived near a school. And they needed a girl
      to help them.

Unalaska Village

I tell Pari, "We have a hospital, a post office, restaurants, a
   movie theater, a store so big you could maybe fit half
   of Kashega inside it." Pari looks away, jealous.
"The men work as fishermen," I say, "in construction,
   as longshoremen and hunters. We have a
   deputy marshal and a commissioner.
We have a church, a beautiful church, which the Golodoffs
   care for like a blessed child."
"And how do they care for you?" Pari asks.

Life in Unalaska Village

"All our childrens are dead," the Golodoffs told me. "We are
   old people. We need someone to look out for us."
I clean for them. I carry and chop and fetch for them. I weave
   fresh grass rugs for them.
And they teach me to make things their way, like the seal-gut
   pants and the seal-gut coats, and they tell me stories
   every night. We are rich enough and we are happy
   enough
And I am away just for a little while to visit my mother and
   my friends in Kashega
      when the Japanese change everything.

EVACUATION
June 1942

ATTACK

Alfred's family was preparing to leave for their summer
      fish camp.
I was going with them, leaving Pari, leaving my mother to
      stay in Kashega and watch over Solomon's store.
But in the endless light of June
The Japanese stung from the sky.

EVACUATION

I try to tell the military that I am not from Kashega, that I am
    only visiting, that my people, the Golodoffs, are in
    Unalaska village and are they okay? And I have to go
    to them.
But the military says my mother is from Kashega. I am from
    Kashega. The twenty of us from Kashega join with
    seventy-two Aleuts from Nikolski, forty-one from
    Akutan, eight from Makushin, eighteen from Biorka.
In shock, we clutch our suitcases and blankets.
On the SS *Columbia* the wind plucks at us. The sinew of
    government laces us to the ship's rail. "We are
    moving you to save you," the government tells us. "With
    your people safely out of the way, our fighting men
    will be free from the worry of you."
    Our ancient roots suddenly exposed,
    even Alfred's mother
    is scraped raw.

In Shock

We gather on the deck. My mother presses me to tell about
  the barbed wire in Unalaska village,
About the nights with our windows covered in tar paper.
  How we couldn't pick the salmonberries or the
  blueberries or the mossberries because they were
  inside the military fences and we were locked out.
I tell how we dug foxholes and bomb shelters because we
  were told to do so by our government. And how
  the rumors flew. About white women and children
  being sent away, but
Alexie and Fekla never believed it would come to this.

At Least We Are Not from Atka

The people from Nikolski say the U.S. Navy, to prevent the
    Japanese from having any advantage,
Splashed fuel
Down Atka walls, across Atka floors, over Atka boats, inside
    the Atka church.
And with the strike of a match everything, everything, the
    entire village, burned to the ground.

STRICKEN

Alfred's grandmother is at my side. "Two hundred years
    ago," she says, "our people lived outside the concern
    of white men; Aleuts were fishermen, seal hunters,
    sea riders.
Then Russians came. Then Americans. Now Japanese, and
    bombs drop through openings in the fog, Japanese
    take control of our islands, and without any say we
    are herded under this bulging tent of war."
Our villages empty of Aleuts, and all along the windswept
    chain the islands grieve for the loss of our laughter.
I look into Alfred's grandmother's eyes and recognize there
    the Bering Sea, which is no more, no less, than an
    ancient woman pacing in her dark robe.

WRANGELL

July 1942

And So It Begins:
The First Stop on Our Journey

In this temporary camp surrounded by trees on the
     grounds of Wrangell Institute
We have little else but the alphabet.
And so we gather together, five villages of Aleuts,
     and start stringing up the lanterns of our lives,
Story by story.

WHO WE WERE

Alfred's grandfather says, "Aleuts have been poets and artists.
We have made music.
We have guided the church and charted the sea.
Now we are trapped like the foot of a bird in the snare
        of war."

We were not so different, dressed in our Western clothes
        brought by the supply boats from Outside, washing
        laundry, cooking on stoves, sitting around the table
        talking.
Except that in every direction the sea surrounded us. Fierce
        winds boxed with us, like prizefighters sprung from
        four corners.
The fog carried us through the treeless hills in her fat arms,
        our faces pressed against her damp skin.
We were not so different. Except that we lived on the margin
        of a continent, content.

WRANGELL SUNSET

The little children have no lice, but still a nurse shaves their
        heads and smears their scalps with kerosene.
We spend the afternoon scrubbing pale skin clean.
The sinking sun sets fire to the clouds,
Our eyes reflect the blood red of a seal hunt.

TEMPORARY SHELTER: THE INSTITUTE

During the school year
The Alaska Indian Service sends older native children here,
    mostly from the mainland, boys in one wing, girls in
    the other, away from their families, their villages,
    their traditions.
Here native children learn to ply the tools useful in the white
    man's world.
But it is summer and the native children have scattered to
    drink in the light of their fish camps. Now this place is
    our refuge, where Aleut men sleep, restless, in
    dormitory beds, and we women and children huddle
    outside, under canvas tents.

Wrangell Dawn

The rain descends, falling straight from a low sky,
Tapping against the tarpaulin, everything damp.
The big white school an island—
      our tents, cloth boats, tied at its shore.
But tents are not boats, and a grassy field is not the
      Bering Sea.

The children complain because we cannot cook breakfast.
Our stomachs twist, hot and knotted. But even if we could
      cook, it is always chum salmon they give us,
      foul-smelling chum salmon.
"Fit for dogs," Alfred's mother says.
"Not Aleuts."

WRANGELL DAY

Dozens of us fill the parlor inside the big school,
Breathing in the smell of polished wood. Innokenty, from
     Akutan, plays Debussy on the upright piano.
Eyes opened, we are Aleuts, exiles, a thousand miles from
     our villages.
Eyes closed, we are sailing toward the Aleutians
     on a rippling sea.

BASEBALL

In Kashega, after a day of fishing,
Alfred and I would put down our lines,
    pick up a rock and a piece of driftwood,
    and mark off the bases in the sand.
Here at Wrangell we play on a real diamond,
    with a rawhide ball and a wooden bat.
And there are enough of us to make two full teams.

WRANGELL NIGHT

Aleut mothers from five villages sing their children to sleep.
From twenty tents rise the good woman voices.
Dark eyes slowly shut: Hard wooden floors
Become the hulls of boats floating in a sea of lullaby.

THE FOOD AT WRANGELL

We eat in the dining room.
Pari complains, "Still dog salmon."
Alfred's mother, Alfred's sister, and I go to help the man
    in the kitchen, maybe season things better.
    Maybe prepare the cheap fish some other way than
    boil.
But the cook says, "There is no other way."

BUILDING THE BARGE

All the men from the different villages are told to
    build a barge
Large enough to carry all of our possessions and a load of
    lumber to Ward Lake.
The government men say that at Ward Lake even the
    barge itself
Will be remade into cabins where we will live
    until it is safe for us to go home.

Catching Cod

Pari says, "Chum salmon, tea, and bread, over and over, each
    day like the day before.
No seagull eggs, no cod, no halibut, no crab,
No salmonberry jam, no blueberry pie, no mussels, no clams,
    no fried bread, no seal."
"Don't," I beg her. "Oh, Pari, don't."

Instead we take turns telling of the time when the tide
    turned and the wind blew the cod to shore.
We ran into the water and kicked the cod onto the beach
    with our bare feet and gutted the cod and feasted for
    days.
But as we remember the harvest of cod we remember too
    how the fish flopped on the beach,
Desperate to get back to the water.

WORKING AT WRANGELL

The women of all the different villages
Come from their tents
To work in the kitchen, the laundry, the bakery,
Even the ones who are sick.

RESISTANCE

Joyfully I watch the arrival at Wrangell of the people from
    Unalaska village.
Alexie wastes no time telling how Fekla squeezed
    under the bed and refused to come out until
    he locked inside a trunk for her all her cups and
    saucers, her silver, the family Bible, all my photographs
    and books.
Until he reassured her I would not return from Kashega,
    thinking they had deserted me. Until
    he dug a good hiding place for all the church
    things. "In the end," he says, "I still had to drag her out
    from under the bed."
I might have coaxed Fekla without so much trouble.

TRAVELING COMPANIONS

Alexie and Fekla managed to bring some clothing, even for
me, and a few icons from the church. "The rest is in
the trunk," they say. "You'll see when we get home."
I do as much for them as I can to make them comfortable
until the government ships them out to Burnett Inlet.
I should go with Alexie and Fekla.
But the government keeps me with the group from
Kashega.

LEVELING THE WORLD OF THE ALEUT

We hear the white people at the Institute talk. They say
    whenever the fog clears over Attu and Kiska,
American fighter planes race out to the very end of the
    Aleutians, releasing their bombs on the Japanese
    intruders.
I tremble beside Eva, imagining American bombs dropping
    like deadly seeds on our emerald earth.
"Oh, Eva," I say, "the bombs are taking root in our place."

THE OUTSIDE MEN

Eva, Pari, and I gather the children into a story circle.
"Long ago," Alfred's grandfather says, "a group of
      whalers jumped ship and, after fighting the cold sea,
      dragged themselves onto the Aleutian shores. They
      grew so hungry, so cold. They killed one of their own
And ate him."
The children climb onto our laps, tunnel their small hands
      into any warm place they can find, and gaze, wide
      eyed, at Alfred's grandfather, as my mother walks past
      with a bucket, laughing.

In Kashega, Alfred's family kept a light burning to warn off
      the *iidigidi*, the bogeymen who roam the Aleutians.
My mother would shake her head at our foolishness, but
      when Pari and Alfred and I were out at night, we
      checked over our shoulders for the Outside men,
Particularly if we had done something to annoy our parents,
      or the church,
Or the white schoolteacher.

39

WORSHIP

One thousand miles away our churches stand empty.
But we are alive and we give thanks.
Five villages' worth of Aleuts gather in the field under a
     steady rain.
The hem of God brushes our upturned faces.

The Value of an Aleut

Pari and I want to go out and gather the dead grass,
To light a cooking fire outside the tent.
This is the Aleut way. On the chain there are no trees,
    driftwood is scarce;
We make fires from bundles of dry grass.

The man from Indian Affairs
Stitches his net around us:
Aleuts go nowhere without permission, he says.
Aleuts go nowhere.

And we submit.
We stay in a bundle at the Institute.
But our dreams are ravens
Flying west over Shoemaker Bay.

WARD LAKE
August 1942–April 1945

Relocation: From Wrangell to Ketchikan

The profiles of islands and tree-covered mountains chew
    jagged bites out of the horizon.
Along the shoreline families carry picnic baskets, taking their
    children on outings under a gray sky.
Our Aleut hands tighten around the metal rail as we
    balance on the *Penguin*'s deck, heading to a new
    evacuation camp;
Fighting the current, the boat noses south into a rain forest,
    farther and farther from home.

Arrival at Ward Lake

Not until we are abandoned in the dark suffocation of the
   forest,
Not until we count only two small bunkhouses and two
   cabins for five villages of Aleuts,
Not until the morning, when we wake, on the floor, a
   landscape of bedrolls and blankets,
Do we discover that we cannot, from any corner of the camp,
   catch a glimpse of open water.

Blanket Houses

We have to choose between warmth
And privacy.
We hang blankets to divide the space inside the crowded
    cabins.
I sleep beside my mother, not quite touching. And we shiver.

Dining at Ward Lake

The kitchen range does the job once the filth left behind by
    the CCC boys has been scoured away,
If we eat our powdered eggs in shifts in the crowded
    mess hall.
But Eva weeps into her bowl,
Remembering her mother's kitchen.

HAMMERING

Our Aleut men begin immediately to saw and hammer and
    shape the planks we towed behind us one hundred
    miles on a barge from Wrangell to Ward Lake.
"Alfred," I say, "maybe without your help the cabins will be
    done quicker." But he knows I am teasing.
We girls and women do our best to bandage the cuts
    of our men, we do our best to mend their bruised
    bodies, but
We have few medical supplies, no healing fox oil. Only our
    ancient skills, our Aleut resourcefulness, and the
    quick chatter of unfamiliar birdsong.

WORMWOOD

Bodies ache. The men are sore from their work.
Alfred's mother sends five villages of girls into the forest. Pari,
    Eva, and I stay close. We move slowly through the
    thick trees, searching for wormwood.
But there is too much green.
We find not a single leaf we recognize.

IMPROVEMENTS

Each new cabin has one small bedroom with bunks, and a
    small kitchen with a camp wood-burning stove.
Our men make everything we need, even the furniture, even
    a fine church and an altar.
The government provides pots, skillets, teakettles,
    heavy dishes.
And we can live here maybe for a little while, but it
    is not home.

MR. WACKER

His face still creased with sleep,
He pulls into camp, opens the doors to his taxi, packs us in,
      collects our fares.
Alfred's grandfather says he is kind to us because we're
      good business.
But my mother heard that Mr. Wacker is married to a native.

OLD TONGUES

In the crowded cabin Alfred's grandfather unlocks the
    ancient box filled with Aleut words.
He spreads before us the stories of Aleut warriors defending
    their fire-breathing islands against invaders.
He says, "We are descended from the fierce Aleut, our home
    is a necklace of jewels around the throat of the Bering
    Sea." That's what Alfred's grandfather says.
But when the men from Ketchikan slip in to sell us liquor,
    they say we look Japanese.

TOO SWEET

We take Mr. Wacker's taxi the eight miles to Ketchikan.
And then we walk, up and down the city hills, past front
    yards and side yards and backyards. Trees are hung
    with ripening fruit: cherry, plum, apple.
Berries swell, hummingbirds and bumblebees *rummm* from
    flower blossom to flower blossom.
The fragrance is too sweet. It makes a throbbing behind
    my eye.

Under a Canopy of Trees

Around our crowded camp, everywhere we turn, green life
    rubs its moss skin against us.
The air steams green, and always the sound of dripping,
Always the smell of rot. Always green curtains smothering us.
On the Aleutians there are no trees.

THE REUNION

What hugging, what shouts of joy
When old friends meet. Alfred's grandfather embraces the
  white family from Ketchikan who ran the little store
  in Kashega for years, before Zachary Solomon came.
I barely remember these friends who bring candy and food
  and clothes and even some medical supplies in the
  back of their car.
But they remember me and offer a store-bought skirt, brand-
  new, and ask about their plantings along the paths of
  Kashega, about the church, and what my mother
  stocked when she ran the store.

PRISONERS OF WAR

Somewhere nearby, we hear, is a camp for German prisoners
    of war.
They are well fed, we hear.
They have cots and blankets, every last one. They have room
    to stretch their long legs. And good sanitation and an
    infirmary.
They are provided a clean, safe place to live, a variety of foods,
    and recreation. They are not expected to contribute in
    any way to their keep.

We are citizens of the United States, taken from our homes.
    We did nothing wrong, and yet we get little to eat and
    no doctoring, and our toilet is an open trough washing
    into the creek.
No seats,
Just a run of water flowing in at one end, flushing waste out
    the other.
The German prisoners and the flies think our
    government has devised a very good system.

CELEBRATION

The men finish all the new cabins. My mother and I move
    into one with Alfred's family.
I look around the camp, so dark, with the trees pressing in.
What else can we do?
Pari and I decide to hold a dance.

THE ROAD TO KETCHIKAN

As dawn birds trill,
My spirit rises with the sun, which parts the fingers of trees
And slides its light through to the forest floor.
Mr. Wacker's taxi pulls up early to carry us to Ketchikan for
    the day.

We ride, Pari, my mother, and I, shoulder to shoulder, the taxi
        smelling of old leather, tobacco, and wintergreen.
The road leans against the channel, alive with
Eagle flight and motorboats and the roar of a
        bush plane skimming over our heads
        on its way to a landing,
Where it will be as welcome as sunlight.

WHILE THE LITTLE ONES PLAY KICK THE CAN

Alfred's grandfather says, "Remember, we were once
    unparalleled hunters, men of the sea.
We were the elders of the world.
We had our own language, our fierce victories, our
    tribal pride.
The Russians ended that.

"We went from ten thousand to eight hundred. Our
    grandparents perished. Our parents perished.
And that was before the
    Americans came.
How many times can a people lose their way
Before they are lost forever?"

Keeping Clean

At Ward Lake we have a laundry.
Four faucets with cold running water emptying into a
tin tray.
We heat water on our little cabin stoves and carry the water
to the laundry house, where
We scrub our clothes over washboards.

The children run in and out of the shower stall at the end of
the building,
Their wet feet slap against the wood floor.
Alfred's grandmother complains.
She misses her steam bath.

FINDING WORK

Now that we have a place to live, the Indian Service reminds
    us that we must find ways to support ourselves.
At home we needed no help. At home we had our boats and
    the sea. We had our fish lines and the kelp beds, we
    had our islets and the murre eggs.
At home we had the wind to re-create the world and its
    offerings each morning.
My mother does not have the money for Mr. Wacker's taxi.
    She walks the eight miles to Ketchikan and goes
    inside every shop and asks if they need help. "I'll do
    anything," my mother says.

Two New Aleuts

Within hours of each other, two baby girls enter the world at
    the Ketchikan public hospital, daughters of women
    from our Aleutian villages.
The people of Ketchikan handle these new lives tenderly.
But when they are brought back to camp, the people of
    Ketchikan forget them.
And these new ones join the struggle along with
    the rest of us.

LETTER TO A P.O. BOX IN SEATTLE

Pari writes to her father in care of the boat he works on out
of Seattle. She tells him about life in the camp.
I sit on the step below her and look back up at her face,
her hands.
Pari twists on the step, the paper on the tread beside her, the
pen skipping over the wooden contours of the step,
Pari skipping over the contours of her family's
separation.
She is so full of longing, no one passing Pari can hold his
heart safe in its velvet box, especially not Alfred.

Idle Hands

In Kashega a dozen empty flour sacks are folded neatly under
    Eva's bed.

If we'd remained in the Aleutians through the summer, we
    would have filled those sacks, gathering the wild grass,
    curing it, sorting it for winter work.

The blades would have waited, carefully encased in clean
    white cloth, until the fierce teeth of the Aleutian
    winter clamped down.

Then, putting aside our knitting, I in my village, Eva and her
    mother and grandmother in theirs, we would have
    brought out the grass and woven thimble baskets.

KETCHIKAN COLD STORAGE

Our men are finding jobs with Mr. Wacker's help.
There's the promise of work maybe even through
    winter.
Some have hired on to build the Creek Street Bridge.
The rest leave early each morning for Ketchikan Cold
    Storage and bring halibut heads home at night
    for us to cook.

The Sting of *Pootchky*

A group of women from two or three villages crowd together
into our cabin.

The talk turns to the old food.

Alfred's grandmother tells about the time Pari and I ate the
celery-like stalks of *pootchky* without peeling them and
burned our mouths with sores that hurt for days.

The women all nod and share stories of their own, and I need
to leave because memories of the Golodoffs pile up
like waves and threaten to drown me.

THE TERRIBLE BEAUTY OF NIGHT

Escaping outside to the cabin steps,
Dim lights burning up and down the row,
Alfred and I sit back-to-back and I tremble to be so near him,
    forgetting for a moment the forest and its thousand
    unnamed monsters, and Pari.
"Don't be afraid," Alfred says, sounding like an old man. I put
    my hand over my eyes so the light he makes shine
    inside me won't leak out.

COMEUPPANCE

A group of us leave the camp before dawn with our homemade
   fishing lines and follow the path to the cove.
The sun rises and touches the mountains across the channel
   with rosy light.
The mists of morning smell different from dawn on the
   Aleutians.
We carry home two freshly caught fish, and one, in the
   throes of death, slaps Alfred on the back, three times
   with its strong tail.

FISH CAMP MEMORY

As I walk behind the others I remember gathering berries
      and grass, and how Alfred, Eva, and I walked across the
      backs of
Salmon churning and driving and spawning in the Milk River,
How our night nets glistened in the moonlight
And the salmon splashed water diamonds into the air.

A FIND

Alfred leads all the children along a path under the giant,
　　dripping trees and finds a beach, where a fledgling
　　chickadee blinks up at us with bright eyes.
Lifting the bird in her hands, one of the smallest children
　　races back through the forest and places the tiny bird
　　on the floor of her cabin where we crowd around,
　　dripping.
The little ones want to keep the chick for a pet; we all miss
　　the pets we left behind in the evacuation.
But the adults tell us we must put the bird back where we
　　found it.

PLAYGROUND

The children do as they did at home.

They give chase, play tag. Bare-legged, they jump from puddle
to puddle.

Only, here their playground is a forest always closing in on
them.

Inside it the sun's light is painted green and the children grow
pale from breathing unripe air.

Disturbance in the Harmony of the Spheres

Mr. Wacker says he read in the paper that along the Aleutian
    chain the volcanoes are restless.
Smoking lava flows down their sides.
Rock and ash rain down on the distant islands.
When I tell Alfred's mother, she says, "It is nature
    holding a mirror up to the troubles of man."

TAXIMAN

Sometimes
Mr. Wacker's cab is so crowded,
The children get home
By riding on the fenders.

So Mr. Wacker trades in his cab for a small bus to carry us to
    and from Ketchikan.
That way, more Aleuts can work outside the camp and still be
    home at night with their families.
Mr. Wacker raises bail when some of our boys get in trouble
    and end their week in the city lockup.
How can we ever repay him, when we Aleuts owe
    Mr. Wacker so much more than bail money?

KETCHIKAN CREEK

When Eva returns from Ketchikan, she says
The creek there is like a woman
Dressed in a filmy green gown,
Her lace pockets spilling with leaping salmon.

Dance Lessons

In our crowded cabin, Alfred and his friends come
    to practice their dancing.
There is just room enough for six clumsy feet.
Pari and I sing for them and teach them to follow the music.
We laugh when they offer us real money, but they say,
    "Take it."

Last Spring's Egg

Alfred, Pari, and I slip out of camp and follow the path
    through the woods.
There we find an abandoned grouse nest with a single,
    unhatched egg.
It is perfect in its buff-colored smoothness and past any
    possible usefulness.
Pari is coughing today. She walks back to camp slowly, leaning
    on Alfred.

CHICKWEED

Chickweed grows along the road to Ketchikan.
Eva and I pick it, cook it, or use it as a salad green.
Something as simple as chickweed carries the taste of home.
And the promise of healing.

SURVIVAL

Alfred gathers us and tells a story. He says, "When my
  grandfather was stranded and hungry on the
  Aleutian trapping grounds,
He used his knife to cut a flap in the sod and, peeling it back,
  slipped beneath, pulling the clammy earth up around
  his chin like a blanket.
With patience he waited for birds to land on top of him.
  Then, quick, he'd reach out and snap their necks."
Alfred's eyes flash with humor as he speaks, and I know what
  his grandfather will say if I ask about this story, but the
  others sit quietly and imagine the small bones in the
  neck of the Japanese.

STICKS

One of Alfred's friends spends the evening balancing sticks
    on the back of his hand,
Tossing the jumble up under the lamplight,
Plucking the black stick out of the air with thumb and
    forefinger, like magic, so quick, leaving
    twenty plain sticks to fall.
The sound of their landing is like the *ting, ting* of hollowed
    bones dropping to Earth.

Rusting

The deer move freely through these chilling woods.
If our men had guns, they could hunt, we could get our own
      food and not rely so much on handouts from the
      government.
But we are not given guns, and our own are rusting in our
      Aleutian homes.
The deer has more freedom to feed itself than we.

MENDING GEAR

At the edge of camp a great pile of fishing gear appears,
Gathered by the government from the people of Southeast
  Alaska.
Donated for our use.
Our men begin to mend the reels, yearning for boats with
  motors, discussing how to keep us all fed in this place
  of trees.

School

The damp chill of autumn sets in, and I want to go to
      Ketchikan High so I can keep studying but still come
      back each afternoon to help out.
Mrs. Whitfield says if I wish to continue my schooling, I have
      to go to Wrangell, to the Institute, where native
      children go
And never come back until next summer.
I talk this over with the elders from the five villages. In the
      end I take a job in the laundry at the Ketchikan
      hospital instead of finishing school.

Pari wants to come with me,
But she still has a cough and they won't hire her.
She follows me with her eyes when I leave for work each
      morning; I see part envy shining there, part relief.
Pari is embarrassed to be Aleut in the streets of Ketchikan.

NATIVE EXPECTATIONS

We have not seen the sun in two weeks.
Not even the quick glimpse that comes when the sky
    repositions its grip on the clouds.
At home the rain, the fog, the winds were familiar. Here the
    weather traps us; we are caught in the tight cage of
    Southeast with bad food, bad sanitation, bad
    medicine.
A military doctor comes from Outside. He is surprised we
    dress as he dresses. "Where are your reindeer skins?"
    he wants to know.

GIFTS

We don't know if we should thank Mr. Wacker
Or Alfred's grandfather's friends,
But someone put a plea for help in the *Alaska Fishing News*,
And boxes of clothes and toys and books pour into camp.

On the Island of Unalaska

The flowers have closed their mouths and begun their
    descent into winter sleep.
Snow comforts the shoulders of Mount Newhall,
A brown jumble of chest-high grasses rasps and scrapes in the
    williwaw winds,
And the blowfly puzzles over the absent hunter who, like a
    god, every autumn until now, provided a feast of fresh
    kill.

Unalaska Memory

Last year, in Unalaska village, when the fierce wind played the
    grass like a tempest of green violins,
When the waves crashed against the rocks and the spume
    rose like raging sea lions,
When the snow turned to sleet, the sleet to rain, the rain to
    hail, the hail back to snow again,
I did not know I loved Alfred.

THE POLICE

Maybe they don't like the way we look, out so early on the
     streets of Ketchikan, eager to work any job at the
     hospital, in the canneries, on the fishing boats.
Maybe because we laugh easy, have a good time wherever
     they find us. Maybe because the mayor says we are
     unsanitary and diseased and obnoxious, a dangerous
     menace to his community of white people. Maybe
     because our latrine ruined their sparkling lake.
Maybe that's why they keep taking us to jail and fining us ten
     dollars and ten dollars and ten dollars,
Money we need to feed the little ones.

REQUESTS

Pari's mother says she will write letters to the Indian bureau,
    every day, until they are annoyed enough to listen.
She will ask for a doctor and medicine enough to care for all
    who are ailing in this dark, forbidding forest.
She will ask for better sanitation so we can drink the water,
    breathe the thick air without fear of the illness that
    pins us to our beds.
Pari's mother will not ask to be reunited with her husband.
    Even she knows what is impossible.

SIMPLE QUESTION

The Japanese have been defeated on Attu,
They have retreated from Kiska,
We Americans have retaken the Aleutians as our own again.
May our people go home now?

UNWANTED GUESTS

Walking to work this morning, I overhear men speaking
    behind me. They say Aleuts are no good, they want us
    to move to another location, away from Ketchikan.
We are only trying to survive our exile, I want to say.
Yet our white neighbors scratch at the rash of our existence.
We didn't ask to come here. The Japanese are no longer a
    threat. Let us leave. Let us go home.

BOILS

Nearly everyone in the camp has developed boils,
Eruptions of the skin, painful, angry lesions.
We ask for a doctor, we beg for a doctor to come to us.
When he finally arrives, he tells us we are not ill, only
    "adjusting."

BUMBLEBEE HOUSES

Alfred walks me the eight miles to work, past the late-
    autumn stubble beside the channel.
"In Kashega," I tell him, "Pari and I pretended the blue lupine
    blossoms were bumblebee houses." Alfred laughs,
    remembering our old games, our old ways.
Alfred's grandmother remembers too. She says the boils on
    our skin can be healed with wild geranium, with
    ragwort, with all the old Aleut medicine, but
When I say this to a girl I work with at the hospital,
    she laughs.

TREES

The elders from Nikolski tell of the time before the white
men came, when a single tree grew in the Aleutians
and the Aleutian sparrow sang as it flew around the
ascending trunk.
The seasoned tree proudly wore its struggle for life, and it
alone reached up through the fog into the heavens.
The Russians chopped the tree down and built their Aleutian
homes from its wood, and all those who touched the
wood of that tree and lived in those homes met an
early and mysterious death.
Here in our Southeast camp there are a thousand trees, but
where is the Aleutian sparrow?

Discrimination

We have become an endless hunger,
A bottomless need.
There is frost on the faces of our hosts, frost our innocence
    cannot melt.
And trouble advances like lava.

WET

Our books ruined because the pages are too wet to turn.
    Everything stinks of mildew.
Our blankets, our hair. Our skin never dries, our clothes
    cling, our feet are damp, we are always coughing.
Perhaps somewhere people sleep in dry beds
And take the sunlight for granted.

LULLABY

We sang to her when she fretted in the gray morning,
We sang to her as we carried her back and forth across the
    cabin floor,
We sang to her in the night when a cough stiffened her
    infant body.
Our music, which could lull a healthy baby to a night of
    sweet dreams, carried her, wrapped in the many voices
    of our people, back to the house of the
    innocents.

TRADING

The Aleut does not always get the good end of a trade.
Once, the Aleuts piled sea otter skins until they reached the
    top of a Russian gun.
The Aleuts kept the gun, the Russians kept the skins. This
    time we trade our skin of freedom for the gun of the
    government's protection.
Even the Russian trade was better than this.

Akutan Girls

The girls from Akutan say when the seal hunt brought in
    little, they knew well the size of their stomachs.
Here at least powdered eggs are provided, and canned
    rations.
A guardian watches over us, keeping danger away.
And there is a certain beauty to these thick trees, these deep
    carpets of vegetation, this odor of leaves.

GOING TO THE MOVIES

Pari and Alfred and I can't afford the taxi ride. We have
    money enough only for admission to the movie.
But we all three need to get out of camp.
So we walk eight miles to Ketchikan and eight slow miles
    back home again
Where I gently put Pari to bed because she
    is unable to do it for herself.

WITH LIBERTY AND JUSTICE FOR ALL

We pray and hug one another in our rumpled bunks, and the
    light from the cabin shines on the smooth-faced yard.
Mr. Wacker posts bail and brings my mother back from the
    Ketchikan lockup, where she was being held,
Accused of selling favors.
We whisper late into the night; snow falls softly, filling the
    broken paths.

BIORKA BOYS

Alfred's friends from Biorka talk. "When we were small," they
    say, "always we heard stories. The elders called us in,
    even on sunny days, to tell stories.
Our ears learned to listen, even as we pretended indifference.
    Even as we slept, stories washed over us.
Every day our eyes tracked the strong hands of our fathers;
    even as they sat at the table mending their gear, they
    told their stories.
But in this relocation camp, their stories drop like stones into
    the sea."

HOUSE-HUNTING IN KETCHIKAN

My mother pays her thirty-five cents and rides the taxi-bus to
    Ketchikan.
She does not wear clothing from the barrel of discards
    donated to us by the generous of the town. She wears
    clothes she has bought on her own.
On the streets of Ketchikan all the citizens are buttoned into
    their wool coats and hats. And each booted foot
    climbs up long steps to home.
My mother finds a room for one, "only one," she says, not
    meeting my eyes. "It's well heated." She sighs and I
    have never felt more forsaken.

THE POWER OF MUSIC

If our men had known how much we would need music in
    this camp, if they'd been given the time to gather
    what is important to an Aleut,
They would have brought their guitars along with their
    bedrolls when they boarded the evacuation ship.
Before the war they traveled from village to village playing
    Aleut music, and we danced and laughed, and the
    little ones curled into sleep atop the thick piles of
    warm coats.
Now, silent guitars lean in the corners of Unalaska homes,
    but the men still have their voices with them and
    their songs. When we dance, we forget to shiver in
    the Ketchikan cold.

DARTS

Alfred's grandfather carves darts and a fish for us, and we play
    in Pari's cabin while she watches from her bunk.
The boys are best at spearing the fish in its belly for the
    highest score.
I could hit the belly maybe, but I aim for the fish's eye,
    earning few points but much laughter.
Alfred teases more than the others, then like a shy crab, he
    scuttles out the cabin door.

Digging Clams in December

We layer every piece of donated clothing onto our bodies
And head to the beach, moving in a thoughtful line through
    the white-cloaked forest, our empty sacks tossed over
    our shoulders.
With improvised shovels and rakes, with our worn soles, we
    dig the sweet, juicy clams,
Acting out the ancient clam digger story, the rise and fall of
    our shadows, a bobbing sea of Aleuts in the
    moonlight.

PROMISE

"When can we go home?" the little ones ask
    as the temperature drops colder than we have ever
    known it on the Aleutians.
"The salmon go home each year," they say. "And the seal. . . .
    When can we?"
Alfred's grandfather makes no promises, he looks at his
    cracked shoes and shakes his head.
Pari, who is feeling better, tells the children, "Listen. We will
    make a Christmas star."

GLUE

We cut out the pieces for the Christmas star and ask Mrs.
    Whitfield for glue, but she cannot spare a drop.
So we go to Alfred's grandfather, and he tells us to catch
    four cod,
Boil their eyeballs in water, crush the cooling goo with our
    fingers, and use that for glue.
The next day, on my way home from the hospital laundry,
    I stop in town and buy glue from the store.

CHRISTMAS AT KASHEGA

We waited for the mail boat to bring the fresh-cut Christmas
    greens to the treeless Aleutians.
If the mail boat was late, we had no tree to decorate. But
    Alfred's grandfather gave out bags of popcorn and
    homemade toys.
And eventually the mail boat came, bringing Santa and his
    sack of apples.
Here we have Christmas greens in every cabin, and we wait
    not for Santa, but for permission to go home.

GROWING WINGS

Someone from Ketchikan donated a worn pair of lace
    curtains.
We washed them, cut them to shape,
And used starch to form them
Into angel wings for the children.

SEARCH

All the girls sit in a circle, with Alfred standing in the center.
Slyly we pass the bundle of knotted cloth under our spread
    skirts, secretly slipping it from girl to girl.
At last Alfred chooses. He says, "Vera is hiding the bundle."
    And for the first time, as I show my empty hands, I
    see it is me Alfred loves, not Pari. Pari sees too.
The other girls rise, laughing at his mistake, and beat him on
    the back until he stalks away.

Northern Lights

The crowded cabin sighs and snores and moans with sleep
    sounds.
Restlessness brings me outside,
To the steps.
I sit alone in wonder.

Spinning Star

Pari is relieved. She says Alfred likes the old ways too much.
    We draw Aleutian flowers on
The four-foot-tall paper star, with its eight points spinning
    around a stationary center.
There is no anger in her heart as she draws the Nativity scene,
    there is no anger in her heart as I surround her
    drawing with a crown of paper flowers.
The children are proud of this new star we've made, but Pari
    and I remember the star of glass a thousand miles
    away, waiting in the back room of the Kashega
    church.

CHRISTMAS

Twenty-two of us walk from cabin to cabin in the snowy
     night,
Singing our ancestral hymns.
Our footsteps fill in quickly under the low sky.
It is hard to believe on every continent a war is raging.

SEPARATION

Some of our boys have joined the fighting.
They send money back to us. All of our money is pooled
    together, all of it, from all five villages.
Some families have left the camp for good, gotten permission
    to live in Ketchikan, that city of steps and liquor,
    gardens and canneries, tunnels and cloudscrapers.
My mother was one of the first to leave.

RUSSIAN ORTHODOX CHRISTMAS

We carry in the sick ones and bring chairs for them.
The rest of us stand in the unheated church, decorated with a
    hundred paper flowers, made in the kitchen near the
    stove over the past weeks.
The chanting lasts for nearly three hours.
And at the end we each press our lips against the holy
    picture, even the babies.

THE RUSSIAN NEW YEAR

When the time comes,
I look inside myself. I wonder what awaits me in the new
    days. Everyone else, it seems, has known about Alfred
    all along. Since before I left Kashega for Unalaska
    village. And I never saw it.
The night before the Russian New Year we dress up and
    dance and have a good time. Loud and joyful. Alfred
    and all the boys take turns dancing with me and Pari
    and five villages of girls.
At midnight we stop dancing, start praying, hard, and even here
    our prayers reveal a thousand reasons
    to be grateful for another year.

We have no guns to fire off at dawn,
But the noisy chatter of the magpie makes us laugh
    at ourselves and
Our proud little camp
In the dense forest, under the pale light of the winter sun.

COLD SHOULDERS

In town they hold meetings. Should they move us, should
    they let us stay?
In our camp the boys want to dance like Outsiders, like
    cheechakos,
They want to be like the men in movies.
We shiver in our hand-me-down clothing and wonder at how
    quickly the goodwill of the season unravels.

117

ESCAPE

Some Aleuts have found a way out of their grief.
Nothing hurts when the body is numb with drink.
Money that might have bought fresh fish or game or a sweet
    for the children
Buys instead liquor to grease the rusting Aleut engine.

PATHS

An eagle cries overhead. We cannot see him through the
    snow-bowed trees.
The men do their heavy-footed dance between the cabins,
Tamping down paths so that we will not be cut off from one
    another.
The road leading out of camp is marked by nothing
    but the delicate tracings of a wren.

SNOW STORY

Snowfall brings the shouts of children at play.
We follow the sound through the forest and come to Ward
    Lake Recreation Area, where happy sledders set a
    chiming of joy resounding through the
    snowpacked trees.
We remember the wind on our cheeks and our own sled
    mornings, before school, when the world was
    fastened inside its white coat.
But now the coat belongs to these other children, and we
    watch from the shadows.

CHURCH SONG

Our voices blend and rise like the dough for the *alaadik*.
The sound is fragile, easily flattened by the heavy hand of this
    refugee life,
But the church contains us like a good bowl, and we warm
    one another as we stand close together,
And the guard from Ketchikan who watches over us
    turns hungry ears to the sweet music
    floating through the mist of winter forest.

FEVER

So many ill. Fevered, with TB, with pneumonia. Asleep in our
    sweat, too weak to eat, and coughing, all of us.
In our nightmares Death rows through the thick trees to the
    shore of our camp.
We are too sick to prepare our dead for their graves, too sick
    to sit with their cold bodies through the long night.
We are floating on the clouds of our dreams, hovering above
    the damp forest floor, and the burning candles in the
    church ignite thousands of paper flowers.

TERRITORY

We have our own cemetery here. It is all that is truly ours,
    and each month it gets a little larger.
Pari's mother says if she dies in this place, we must carry her
    bones back to the Aleutians when we go home,
    because here sometimes the bodies float out of their
    graves and are eaten by bears.
Pari's mother misses my mother's friendship. She worries
    about my mother.
It is Pari I worry about.

MENACE

We are called undesirables and told we must leave
    Ward Lake.
In the time we have been here twenty have died.
Twenty more shipped Outside
To TB hospitals.

Out on the Aleutians some cheechako soldiers are going crazy.
Khaki-wacky, they call it. Aleutian stare, they call it.
    The soldiers feel isolated, abandoned by our
    government, bored, betrayed. They are
    taking their own lives.
It is hard for us to understand. They are in our homes, our
    villages, our churches. They have electric lights,
    running water.
All the comforts.

We have worked hard to improve the camp.
Purchased war bonds
With money we might have used for food.
Yet we are called a menace and told to leave.

We didn't choose to come here.

We have complied because our government asked this of us.

Don't send us to yet another camp where even more will die,
    where our entire people will die.

Let us go home.

PATIENCE

Aleuts fear little. At home we have faced the powerful wind,
    which carries off a roof or moves an iron stove across a
    room.
We have been shaken by earthquake and volcano, smothered
    by fog that swallowed the path, leaving only the high
    squeal of gulls and an anguished sea and a screaming
    wind to fill our senses.
But we have always known that the sun would tear through
    the sheets of storm-tattered clouds,
The way the Aleut child tears through wrapping paper to
    find the doll that has come off the supply ship
    after months of waiting.

BAKING A BIRTHDAY CAKE

We knock on Mrs. Whitfield's door.

It is Pari's birthday. We can bake her a cake if we can have
    some sugar and shortening and flour and vanilla and
    coconut.

We carry the ingredients to the kitchen.

Perhaps in every town, in every village, in every place people
    live together, in every part of this world, it is
    someone's birthday and someone else is baking them
    a cake and singing.

At Pari's Bedside

She won't take even a sip of water. I wet my finger and touch
    it to her chapped lips.
Her hands are cold in spite of the fever.
I read to her from the Sears and Roebuck catalog my
    mother sent.
And later, in the dark cabin, I hum the Slavic hymns. Pari's
    breath comes less and less often.

LOST

Long ago Pari and I went everywhere together. We rowed out
and gathered eggs, we climbed up into the hills, into
the fog, into the wind.
Pari would link arms with me, and we'd go together,
surefooted, laughing.
We floated together in the hot springs, naked, with the stars
bright above us, and slept in the old *barabara*, the
ancient dwelling place we discovered dug into the
hillside. The ghosts of our Aleut grandmothers
whispered stories to us there.
Now Pari's ghost must find its own way back to the fire pit
and keep company with nothing but shadows.

Escape II

Grief turns me invisible as I walk out of camp, down the path.
Water stretches between this shore and the wooded mountains
    across the channel.
The air is fur thick, damp and green.
I sit on the sand in the rain,
    and I scream.

A Reminder

Alfred finds me.
He puts his arm across my shoulder and
Walks me back to camp.
"Everyone is grieving," he says.

BURIAL

Jagged as a broken comb,
We stand around the raw earth, with its
    unblinking eye staring up into our dark faces.
We chant as the body is lowered.
A sudden slant of sunlight breaks through and rests its warm
    palm on our heads.

SEAL KILL

The longing to return to the Aleutians brings our men
To the front of the line, volunteers for the Pribilof seal kill.
The quota from our camp quickly fills.
Alfred watches as his father leaves, envious, but I am glad
Alfred will stay.

What Is Familiar

The evening gathers women and children into its arms.
  Grandmothers weave their baskets.
We older girls play chess or help the little ones piece together
  the jigsaw puzzles given us by the children of
  Ketchikan.
I read aloud from the *National Geographic,* and we take turns
  looking at the pictures of camels.
We grow accustomed to our exile.

LESSONS

The oldest of the grandmothers grows weaker each day.
Yet each day she sits up, if only for a few moments, and
    teaches us to weave the baskets from raffia.
Even the girls who want to stay in Ketchikan after the war, for
    money, for jobs, for a modern life,
Even they pay attention.

ALMOST EASTER

We turn a corner.
Eva finds the strength
To sit up in her bunk
And ask for clams.

We paint Easter eggs with school supplies, brushes and
pots of paint.
We bake Easter bread, *kuliich*, and ice it with sweet
white glaze.
In our little church we have grown used to the absence
of our Bibles, our icons. Instead we form a procession
and follow the American flag around the room.
The chanting lasts for hours.

We are wearing the nicest clothes from the donation boxes,
Moving from cabin to cabin, offering to each family
The brightly painted Easter eggs
And sweet slices of frosted bread.

CIRCLING

We have lived in this camp for three years.
These days the tide of despair rarely rises any higher than our
    shins.
Alfred's grandfather
Is teaching the boys to build an Aleut skin boat.

What's in a Name

A suggestion
To change the name of the Aleutians
To General Billy Islands
Rippled the camp with laughter.

Thinking Ahead

Most of us dreamed of going Outside, hungry for a taste of
    life beyond the Aleutians.
Few of us truly meant it, few of us ever really intended to
    leave the fog and the wind, the sun and the rain, the
    hunting and trapping and fishing, the easy welcome
    of neighbors.
We never thought who we were was so dependent on where
    we were.
But when we settle back into the quiet villages along the
    Aleutian beaches, who will we be after all of this?

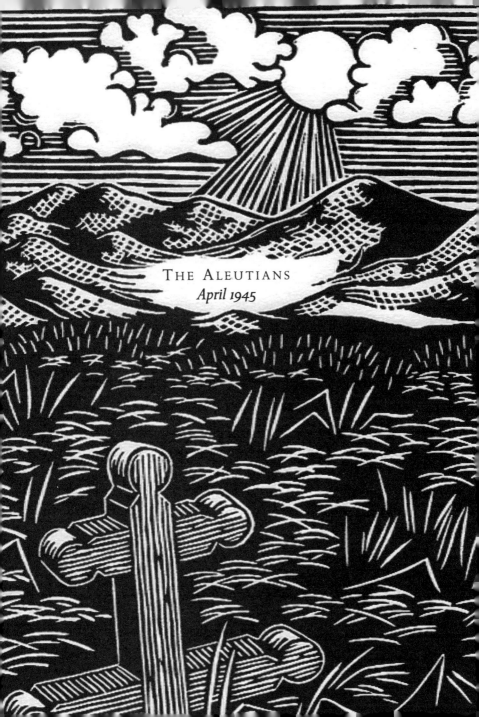

THE ALEUTIANS
April 1945

LAST LEG

We had a service the night before, and there was such joy,
    knowing, at last, our exile was over. After the service we
    burned our Ward Lake altar, and an elder from
    each village took a handful of ashes with him, to be
    buried back home.
In the morning we boarded the *Branch* and began the last leg
    of our journey.
Three years ago there were so many of us heading into
    Southeast, into the unknown.
    Now we leave too many behind
    as we sail back to the Aleutians.
Someone says they heard Alexie and Fekla
    held on almost to the end. But I refuse to
    believe the Golodoffs are not waiting for me.

No More Kashega

All the Kashega people are told they must live in Akutan now.
   The government will not let the people of Kashega
   return home.
Too much is broken, the government says. Too few Kashega
   people left to fix it. My mother knew all along she
   was finished in Kashega. She remained in Southeast
   with all the others, the dead,
And the living with their jobs, their steps, their Ketchikan
   beaus.
The government allows me to return to Unalaska village, and
   though Alfred's family will start over in Akutan,
   Alfred has chosen to come with me.

Sea Change

After three years of promises we are back
Where the sun emerges from the galloping clouds,
Where one moment the rain ices our hair and the next a
    rainbow arches over the volcano,
Where early grass ripples in the wind and violets lead an
    advance of wildflowers across the treeless hills.

It all comes back so quickly, the particular quality of the air
    where the Bering Sea meets the Pacific.
The Aleutian sparrow repeats over and over its welcome of
    fluid notes.
Our resentment folds down into a small package and is
    locked away under the floor of our hearts.
What other chance do we have to survive if we cannot forget?

HOMECOMING

When we dock in Dutch Harbor,
The army
Will not let us go to our homes. We hear rumors, terrible
    rumors.
But the army makes us stay in Quonset huts behind barbed
    wire.

Beyond the Barbed Wire

I turn to Alfred.
He holds me as the truth about the Golodoffs breaks over my
    head.
Our isolation once shielded us from the greater world.
Where is that protection now?

Returning to Unalaska Village

My chest is tight as I push through the debris that was my
    home. The peeling wallpaper, the rusted stove, the
    broken pipes.
I tell Alfred, "This once was the place I lived with
    Alexie and Fekla.
I wonder if I had been with them, would they still be alive?"
Alfred says, "I wonder if you had not been with me,
    if I would be."

The doors hang open.
All the windows shattered.
The trunk busted; books, bedding, papers, clothing strewn in
    piles, ruined. Alexie's gun and tools gone, the Golodoff's
    marriage certificate stolen off the wall,
Even the seal-gut pants. What does a soldier from Arkansas
    want with seal-gut pants?

Smile for the Camera

A white man comes up.
He points a camera at what is left of my home.
"Hold that cup and look sad," he says.
I drank tea from this cup, sitting across the table from Fekla.

I hoped to find the pictures of me and Pari, of the Golodoffs,
Taken when the world was different,
When everything made sense.
All I hoped for were those pictures and maybe my books. I
    knew I would never see my little skiff. Never
    see my chickens. But there is only this: on a shelf
    in what used to be our kitchen
    an enormous pair of khaki pants with a hole in the
    backside.

The Spoils of War

Our fishing grounds and beaches slick with oil,
Our berry patches crushed under the weight of Quonset
    huts, our churches looted.
We cannot eat the war-poisoned clams and mussels; soldiers
    murdered our foxes and our sea lions.
Our very culture stolen or destroyed, not by the enemy, but
    by our own countrymen.

RESETTLEMENT OFFICER

We need everything the Red Cross warehouse holds.
Everything.
But the Red Cross says those supplies are for emergencies
only.
The resettlement officer scratches his head, removes the lock
from the warehouse door, and walks away. Hours later,
when he returns, he smiles to see how well we have
conducted ourselves in an emergency.

LEFT BEHIND

In Europe care was taken to preserve the places of history.
On the Aleutians holy places collapsed under the bombs, one
    after another, like toy buildings.
And the priceless relics from czarist Russia traveled Outside
    in duffels,
Packed between posters of pinup girls and soiled
    government-issue underwear.

Worldwide
Our government spends large sums of money to piece lives
    back together.
No money is spent here.
War leaves ugly scars.

DIGGING UP THE TREASURE

The old church in Unalaska village survived.
And in the churchyard,
Deep in a pit where Alexie hid them,
So did the holy relics and the seven Russian bells.

PROCESSION

We carried
Pari and her mother home with us
And buried them under the shadow
Of Mount Newhall.

The gulls squeal overhead, and in the harbor
      a murre perches on a half-submerged wreck.
The wind whips our hair across our faces, the sun breaks
      through to touch the grasses on the mountainside,
And as Aleuts have always done,
We find the will to begin again.

AUTHOR'S NOTE

In early June 1942 the Japanese attacked the North American continent, bombing Unalaska Island, located about midway along Alaska's Aleutian (ah-LOO-shun) chain. Within days of these air attacks the Japanese captured and occupied the islands of Kiska and Attu, located at the far western reach of North America. The Japanese bid for control of the North Pacific led the U.S. government to evacuate the majority of Aleut (al-ee-UTE) residents living west of Unimak Island.

Most Americans stationed in the Aleutians during the war behaved honorably and fought bravely against both the Japanese and the harsh conditions of the North Pacific. Some servicemen, however, suffered severely from boredom and depression, contributing, along with weather and neglect, to the destruction of Aleut property.

The occupying Japanese found the Aleutian climate challenging as well. Assaulted by frequent storms and vigorous U.S. military strikes, the Japanese ceased to be a threat in the Aleutians by summer's end, 1943. Still, with the exception of the Pribilof Aleuts, who were allowed to return to Saint George and Saint Paul in 1944, the majority of Aleut evacuees were not permitted home again until the spring of 1945. It is estimated that by that time as many as one in every four evacuated Aleuts had died from tuberculosis, whooping cough, measles, mumps, pneumonia, or pain.

For years the survivors of Southeast Alaska relocation camps remained silent about their ordeal. To this day the rusting debris of abandoned military junk disfigures the Aleutian landscape; certain villages that existed before 1942 have never been repopulated. The damage done in those three years to the Aleut culture is incalculable.

This book is a work of fiction based on true events. The Aleut characters described here are not intended to depict specific individuals, but rather to represent the experience shared by many during the three-year relocation. Time and place have been compressed to facilitate storytelling.

Word choices and Aleut spelling have been selected for readability and to reflect common usage in the 1940s:

alaadik—fried bread eaten with sugar or jam

Americanchin—to become a "white" American

barabara—traditional Aleut sod house

cheechako—disparaging term for people living outside of
 Alaska in the lower forty-eight states

iidigidi—bogeyman or restless spirit

kuliich—glazed bread baked at Easter

pootchky—an edible (when peeled) Aleutian plant

williwaw—hurricane-like wind

ABOUT THE AUTHOR

Karen Hesse is the winner of a 2002 MacArthur Fellowship and the author of some fifteen books for children. A school visit to Ketchikan, Alaska, was the genesis for this book. Her many novels include *Out of the Dust*, the 1998 Newbery Medal winner; *The Music of Dolphins*, an ALA Best Book for Young Adults; and *Stowaway*, a *New York Times* best-seller. Karen and her husband live in Brattleboro, Vermont.